# 3 Man Huddle: MMM Best Friend Romance

Van Cole

Published by Van Cole, 2022.

This is a work of fiction. Similarities to real people, places, or events are entirely coincidental.

3 MAN HUDDLE: MMM BEST FRIEND ROMANCE

**First edition. November 16, 2022.**

Copyright © 2022 Van Cole.

ISBN: 979-8223475378

Written by Van Cole.

# Table of Contents

# 3 Man Huddle
# MMM Best Friend Romance

By: Van Cole

# Foreword

The playboy life is the life for me and nothing is going to change that. Nothing.

That is until I got this wild idea that changed my entire life.

Now, most people wouldn't go gunning for their best friend –

Or, their best friend's ex.

I went for both.

That's right.

Both.

Because, why settle for one when you can have two?

Truth be told, this probably isn't my best nor brightest idea.

And I'm prepared for everything to crash and burn.

Or, at least, I thought I was.

But things are getting heated and I'm getting attached.

I don't want to lose these guys but things don't always work out the way you want them to.

And I have a bad habit of coming up short.

Let's just hope my love life is nothing like my career because one more failed Superbowl and I'm just another failure for the history books.

# 3 Man Huddle

# Chapter 1: Axel

The football rolled off my fingertips and penetrated into the air where it went flying all the way across the field. One of my receivers sprinted after it, trying to time his catch just right. "Come on..." I whispered under my breath. "You can do this. That was a perfect throw."

And just when I thought he was about to miss; the receiver dove toward the ground and hugged the ball tight to his body.

The rest of the team erupted into a cheer.

"Good job, Anderson," I said as I offered him a hand. "Just keep it up when the season starts."

"You can bank on it QB." He spiked the ball into the ground.

I was about to join my team in celebration but before I could take a single step, I was approached by the coach. As always, he wore a stern expression on his face. He was a hard man to please. No matter what I did, he just told me to do better.

"You'll have to work on your speed."

"What are you talking about?" As the water boy walked past, I snatched up a bottle and chugged back the whole thing. Man, booze was good, but after a long practice in the August sun, water was better.

"You took too long to release the ball. When we start facing those big-league teams, you'll be sacked within a second. Don't forget, that's how you blew it last time."

I clenched my jaw, teeth grinding together. "You don't have to keep reminding me."

"Apparently I do." The coach flipped through his clipboard. "You know the schedule –"

"Yes. I'll be here. Don't you worry." I was about to walk away but then I paused to look him in the eye. "You know, instead of wailing on me all the time, why don't you work on defense? They're the ones that are supposed to make sure I have enough time to make that perfect throw."

"The defense is fine," he said.

"Well, I beg to differ." I knew there was no point trying to argue with the guy but I had to get in the last word. So, before he could say anything else, I walked off.

At this point, the locker room was calling my name. Drenched in sweat, I needed a shower – stat!

But there was a pixie of a blonde blocking the doorway. I could tell by the microphone in her hand that she was a local sports reporter.

"Mr. Drake? Just a word, please." She stepped forward.

"Sure, why not?" I shrugged.

"Thank you."

As she took a minute to prepare herself for the interview, I took the liberty of checking her out. She wasn't half bad – not really my type – but after a couple of drinks, I could see myself in bed with her.

"Okay, we're ready," she announced. She spoke with confidence but I could see a certain level of nervousness just underneath the surface.

"Hit me," I said as I rolled back my shoulders and flashed a charming smile. I liked to think of it as my secret weapon. They never see it coming and that's what makes it so effective.

Instantly, the reporter blushed.

Bingo.

She stammered on her first question, forcing us to start anew.

"Just take a deep breath," I told her as I squeezed her shoulder and leaned forward so our faces were but inches apart. "I don't bite... very hard, that is."

She blushed even harder.

Sometimes, teasing was just too much fun.

"Alright, Mr. Drake, I have a few questions to ask you." She was gripping the microphone so hard that her knuckles were a bright shade of white.

"Fire away."

"What everyone wants to know is whether you think you'll take your team to the Super Bowl this year."

"Without a shadow of a doubt," I answered. "I know that my track record isn't very impressive but with the way things are going, I think this year will be a lucky one."

"Now, some people are saying that this might be the result of faulty coaching. Do you have anything to say about that?"

It was tempting. I didn't like the coach but I had enough common sense to know that badmouthing him on TV wouldn't be a good thing. "Not at all. The team is very tight this year. Everyone is working together and its that kind of synergy that will get us to the top."

The reporter nodded her head. She was hanging on my every word. My voice had that effect on people – both male and female. "It sounds like you have all your ducks in a row, Mr. Drake."

"I'd like to think that there is always room for improvement," I said. "So, as the season starts we will adapt to the circumstances and plow our way to victory."

"Well, on behalf of me and my team, I wish you the best of luck." With that, the camera stopped rolling.

"How was that?" I asked.

"Wonderful. My boss is going to be very pleased with it, I think."

"Good." I leaned against a nearby wall and she gravitated toward me like a moth to the flame. "I wouldn't want a pretty girl like you to get in trouble."

"Oh, that's very kind of you." Despite the bombshell body, she seemed to have an innocent streak. I quite liked that about her. She definitely had the potential to be a firecracker in bed.

"Now, this might be a little too forward of me, but do you think I could get your number?"

"M-My number?" she stuttered. "You want my number?"

"I believe I spoke plain English."

"R-Right," she stammered again. "Sure, you can have my number. Absolutely." Her whole face lit up as she rummaged through her bag for a pen and paper. In the end, she handed over a crumpled-up receipt with her number circled. There was even a little heart next to it. "Feel free to call me any time."

"Oh, I will," I said, my voice husky and seductive. I even flashed her a little smile.

She practically melted into the ground.

With a chuckle, I slipped into the locker room, leaving her behind. There, I jumped into the shower. Most of my teammates were already gone, eager to get home on a Friday. Since I lived alone, I wasn't in much of a rush. I know it might sound weird coming from a big, bad quarterback but it gets pretty damn lonely living in a great big house all on my own. Sure, I invite the occasional fuck buddy but its just not the same as real company. They aren't at all interested in watching a movie or grabbing a bite to eat. I mean, usually I'm not either but it's nice to have the option.

My thoughts wandered toward the perfect partner as I lathered my body with soap. The water was on the verge of boiling but that's exactly how I liked it. Steam rolled in every direction.

As per usual, the last thing I washed was my package. I took it in my hand and stroked it up and down. It hardened slightly but not enough for me to consider finishing the job. Sometimes the ol' boy just needed a rest. He gets plenty of action without me jerking off in the shower stall. After all, I was considered the playboy of the league. If I wanted to keep making appearances on magazines, then I needed to keep up the lifestyle.

I considered the journalist. Maybe she would be my next conquest. She was certainly cute but so was the new water boy. Perhaps he'd end up being the better option. Hey, I don't discriminate.

The hot water started to dwindle. "Well, that's my cue," I said aloud as I turned off the shower and wrapped a towel around my waist.

I was just about to start drying myself off when there came a ding from my phone. I picked it up and saw that it was a text from Riley – my best friend. Ever since high school, we had hit it off and we've been inseparable ever since.

"Hey, I want you to meet someone special," said the text.

"Someone special?" I texted back. "Did you finally lose your virginity?" We had the kind of friendship where we were always making fun of one another. It was our way of showing affection.

"Quit it," came his response. "Meet me by the lake so you can meet her."

"Her, huh? I thought you played for the other team."

"Just get your fat ass down here."

"Fat ass? I should kick your ass."

"You couldn't do that even if you tried. We all know that I could school you in fighting any day of the week."

"Please, that's a lot of smack-talk coming from a marine biologist."

"Marine biologists are very reputable members of society."

"Up yours." I ended the text conversation with a surefire win. I chuckled to myself and then a thought crossed my mind. What would it really be like to have fun with Riley? Since we were such good friends, I had never thought of him in a romantic light but in all honesty, he was pretty damn sexy. He had the clean-cut, schoolboy kind of look. He still kept his hair slicked back as he had back in college. Oh, I bet it would be really nice to get it wild – to make him scream.

No, what are you thinking? Riley's your friend not another one of your fuck buddies, came that voice at the back of my head. You would never tap that.

# Chapter 2: Riley

It was one of those nights where the weather was just perfect. With the summer coming to an end, the air had taken on a bit of a chill but it was still warm enough where a light jacket sufficed.

Bark!

My new dog, Missy, fumbled over with a large stick in her mouth. I tried to take it from her but she growled in protest. "How am I supposed to play with you when you give me such a hard time with it?" I spoke as if I expected her to answer me.

Bark!

Finally, I freed the stick and waved it around my head. She bounced from side to side, tail wagging so fast that it displaced some of the fallen leaves.

"Do you want this, girl, do you?" I asked in a high-pitched voice. Missy had come into my life a few days prior and already, I felt like I had known her all my life. The love she was willing to share was exactly what I needed. Despite my last breakup being over a year ago, I still felt the sting of a broken heart. It's hard to mend something that's so shattered.

Growing impatient, Missy jumped on my chest and nearly knocked me over. Knowing she would probably bite my face off next, I threw the stick into the lake. It splashed against the surface and floated there, waiting to be retrieved.

Without an ounce of fear, my dog jumped in after it. Her tail worked like a rudder, propelling her in the right direction. I watched as I leaned back, trying to get comfortable against the trunk of a tree.

Snap!

I turned around, expecting to see someone but from what I could tell, there was no one there. "Hello?" I focused on my sense of hearing but I was only met with silence.

"Boo!"

I nearly shat my pants. "Fuck!"

Axel started laughing, doubled over at my reaction. "You should have seen the look on your face!" He slapped his knee. "Oh, it was priceless."

"Not funny, man."

"Oh, it was hilarious," he corrected. "When did you become such a pussy anyway?"

"Hey, you want to say that to my face?"

Before we could get at each other's throats, Missy returned. She spotted Axel and instantly forgot all about her stick.

"Traitor," I mumbled underneath my breath as she slobbered all over him.

"Was this the little lady you were telling me about?" Axel dropped to one knee and scratched the dog's neck until she had her back leg shaking. "She's gorgeous. What is she? A golden?"

"Right on the money," I said.

"So, I am safe to assume that this is the special someone you were telling me about?" Axel raised an eyebrow.

"Mhm."

He plopped down beside me. "So, you're still single, then?"

"Mhm."

"You know, if you want me to be your wingman, I am more than happy to provide you with my services."

"I don't need a wingman," I said as I laid back and looked up at the darkening sky. "After Cain, I haven't really found anyone that could spark my interest."

"Bullshit."

"It's true."

"There's plenty of hot guys around town. You're telling me that not one single guy has sparked your interest? Does that dick of yours still work?"

"It works just fine, thank you." I shot him a deadly glare. "And how's yours?"

"Fine, just fine," I said with a grin. "In fact, I think I might use it tonight. The teams new water boy is quite the looker."

"The water boy, really? You've lost your touch." It was difficult to imagine Axel going off and fucking just anyone he wanted. To have that kind of friendship – what was it like? I, for one, would never know that liberty. The relationship meant much more than just a good time. If I was going to sleep with someone then it had to mean something.

"You should see him. In fact, I'll let you have first dibs."

"First dibs?" I repeated. "Don't treat me like I'm some sort of charity case. If I wanted to find another boyfriend then I would have done so."

"And yet, you're still single."

I sighed. "It's probably for the best so I can get my head on straight."

"Don't kid yourself," he retorted. "That's just an excuse and you know it. You still haven't gotten over Cain."

"Of course, I have," I said. "It's been over a year." Deep down, I knew it was a lie but I didn't want Axel to think of me as some kind of a crybaby. "I barely think of him anymore."

"But you still do."

"We dated for a long time."

"You can't keep living this way –" He looked like he was about to say something more but Missy nudged his hand. "Alright, alright." He gave in to her begging and threw the stick into the lake. Just like last time, she jumped in after it. "Quite the swimmer, that one."

"Oh yeah. I'm thinking of enrolling her in the doggy Olympics."

Axel crossed his fingers over his legs, hugging them to his chest in something that looked like a yoga pose. For a moment, I was distracted by his body. Axel was one of the most well-endowed people I knew. Everything about him was perfect from the shape of his member to the length of his shaft.

What?

We've taken showers in the same locker room before.

Seeing his junk was inevitable.

Besides, Axel is my best friend. I would never –

"Tomorrow night, we're having a boy's night." Axel's sudden interjection had interrupted my thoughts and just when they were getting good too. "And you don't have a choice in the matter."

"You know I'm not a fan of night clubs." I tried to convince him against the idea but he just wasn't going to listen to me. There was that burning in his eyes that I knew all too well. He would drag me to a club even if I went kicking and screaming. "But I don't really have a choice in the matter now do I?"

"Smart man." He grinned. "I will be at your house around ten. Be ready."

"So, I should plan for eleven then?"

He flashed one of his charming smiles and for the first time, it made my heart beat a little bit faster.

What is going on? I thought to myself as heat flared between my legs and an erection started to form. My length hardened against the crotch of my pants making it very uncomfortable for me to keep sitting the way I was. Am I really getting turned on by my best friend? Clearly, there's something wrong with me right now.

Axel got up and shot me one more smile over his shoulder before disappearing amongst the thicket. Missy whimpered and she would have chased after him had I not grabbed her by the collar and held her back.

# Chapter 3: Axel

The following night.

"That's what you're wearing?" I raised an eyebrow. "I mean, you don't look bad but it's not really what you wear to a club." I tugged on his black t-shirt just to make a point.

"What's wrong with jeans and a t-shirt? Last I checked there wasn't a dress code."

I stepped back and gave him a once-over with my eyes. In all honesty, he looked pretty damn fine. If he hadn't been my best friend, I probably would have picked him up a long, long time ago.

"Throw on a white shirt and a leather jacket."

"What am I, a Greaser?"

"Greased Lightning himself," I said with a grin.

"You've never seen that movie, have you?"

"Nope."

"Sometimes, it blows me away how uncultured you are."

"Uncultured?" I repeated. "I have no idea what you're talking about." As I leaned against the doorframe, he took off his shirt, revealing a nice, lean body.

Mmm.

When did Riley become so hot? I thought to myself. He wasn't always this toned, was he?

I couldn't keep my eyes off him. My heart rolled into action, as it normally did before I lured someone to bed. But this was crazy – Riley was my best friend. I wasn't about to bring him to pound town. That would ruin our friendship...

But then he bent over and I got a really nice view of his backside and I was sprung. To keep my erection from him, I turned slightly in a far-from-natural position.

"What's wrong with you? Do you have to go to the bathroom or something?"

"Now that you mention it..."

"I had to remind you?" Riley asked, unconvinced. "If that's the case, then you might want to get that checked out by a medical professional."

I pegged him off before escaping to the bathroom. There, I splashed my face with a bit of cold water. That was enough to wake up my senses and make me realize that I had completely lost my mind.

Riley wasn't interested and neither was I.

And yet, there was still this tugging at my heart trying to tell me otherwise.

Knock. "Are you alright in there or did you fall in?"

I swung the door back, trying to catch him off guard but all that happened was a near collision of our heads. I was so close to kissing him that I could almost taste his lips against mine. His cheeks reddened as did mine. A flame of emotion burned inside of me. This had never happened before.

"Uh... if you're going to drag me to this club then we had better get going," he said in hopes of diffusing the tension that was building between us.

I nodded with a certain numbness. In all honesty, I didn't know what was coming over me. And, it didn't help that my head was spinning.

Thankfully, the fresh air helped quite a bit. On his front porch, I sucked it in. From behind the door, his dog whimpered. "How are you getting along with your new roommate?" I asked.

"Oh, she's wonderful." A sparkle colored his eyes, turning them a brighter shade. Was this even the same guy I called my friend because, by the looks of it, he had been switched with some Grecian God. It was like I was seeing him for the very first time. "She loves to cuddle."

"Is that so?" I unlocked the car and slipped inside.

"Yeah, I can barely move at night."

"Sounds like a problem."

"I don't mind it. I like feeling her warmth."

I reached over and rested a hand on his thigh. "I'm sorry to tell you this but you sound really pathetic. Like it or not, you really need to find yourself another boyfriend."

"I don't need another boyfriend," he said stubbornly. "I am perfectly fine on my own."

"Is that why you got a dog, then?"

"I got a dog because I happen to like dogs," he retorted. "Last I checked, that isn't a crime."

"No, it isn't a crime," I agreed. "More like a cry for help." I grinned over at him as we eased onto the highway. The car was a smooth ride and without even thinking about it, I was tearing through the speed limit and weaving through traffic.

"Must you drive like a maniac?" Riley clutched at his seat, trying to ground himself against the experience. "One of these days, you're going to crash and burn and I'd rather not be in the car when you do it."

"Would you relax? You're such a stick in the mud, you know that?"

"I'm sorry that I value my life more than you do."

"Live a little."

"I can't live if my brains are scattered on the side of the highway," he countered.

"You're being dramatic."

"You're going 100 in a 65."

"So?"

"So? That's way too fast."

I sighed and eased on the gas until it felt like I was crawling at a snail's pace. "There, is that better?"

"Much."

***

That's the thing about Riley – he likes to play it safe. If I consider myself a gambler then he's the retiree with a 401K, pension plan, and life insurance all bundled up with a bow.

"So, are you going to sit at this bar all night?" I shouted over the blaring music.

"I'm sure as hell not dancing with that mob."

"Come on," I urged but he wouldn't listen to reason. "Just one little dance."

"No."

"Why did I even bring you? You're as stiff as a board."

"You should be asking yourself that. You were the one that insisted I should come along for the ride."

I rolled my eyes. "Well, have fun with your little... martinis.

He chomped down on an olive. "Will do."

Part of me wanted to grab him by the wrist and drag him onto the dancefloor but I really didn't want to go through the hassle of dealing with his hissy fit. If he wanted to drag his feet, then so be it. I wouldn't let him slow me down.

As soon as I felt the vibrations of the music underneath my feet, it fueled a surge of adrenaline. That adrenaline powered my dance moves. I was slick, grinding up against anyone with a pulse.

Hey, I don't discriminate.

A few girls tried to cling on for a dance or two but I wasn't interested in making any sort of commitments that night. No, all I was looking for was a bit of fun.

And that's when I saw him.

Unlike everyone else, he looked put together. His style was tight. The sports jacket matched the pants and the belt matched the shoes. This was a guy that knew exactly how to dress for his body type.

I whistled as I approached him.

"Might I say that you're looking rather fine this –" I didn't finish my compliment because it dawned on me that this man looked oddly familiar. "Wait... you're Cain, right?" After a few drinks, I wasn't sure whether my eyes were playing tricks on me or not. "You look just like my best friend's boyfriend."

"Riley?" he guessed.

"Yeah." I pointed my thumb at the bar. "He's right at the bar. Maybe you two should reconnect."

"Reconnect?" He shook his head. "I doubt that Riley wants anything to do with me after our breakup."

"I never got the details –"

"And now's not the time." He took my hand and laced our fingers together. "Because I would much rather share a dance with the best-looking guy in this place."

And despite the repercussions of running off with my best friend's ex, I just couldn't refuse his invitation.

Our bodies were like two puzzle pieces that had finally found their match. Every move he made, I countered with a mirrored one of my own. My skin felt like a pure sheet of electricity as we fell into perfect sync.

By the end of the techno loop, we were both breathless. The corners of his eyes crinkled with an amused smile. "I didn't know that football players were so good on the dancefloor."

"Just me," I boasted as I puffed out my chest.

"Lucky me, then." He held out what looked like a business card. "If you're ever looking for a good time, you know who to call."

I hesitated. It felt wrong of me to take his digits. A harmless dance was one thing but accepting his card was another. There would be implications behind the gesture and I wasn't sure it was worth jeopardizing my relationship with Riley. What would he think if he found out?

Still, I took the card and slipped it into my back pocket.

"I'll be seeing you around." Cain disappeared a moment later and I was left feeling like it had all been a dream.

Dazed, I walked back to the bar to retrieve Riley and take us home. "I see you've been busy," he said as soon as I was close enough to hear him.

"Hmm?"

"I saw you with Cain." His lips pressed together into a tight, disapproving line.

"I didn't mean anything by it, Riley." I held up my hands in hopes of proving my innocence. "It was just a dance."

"Just a dance," he mumbled underneath his breath. "Yeah, right."

"I swear –"

"I don't need an explanation," he interjected. "All I need is a ride home."

# Chapter 4: Cain

The following morning.

I woke up around eleven and considered making myself some breakfast to cure the hangover that lingered against my brain but there was only one sure-fire method to cure the drinking blues.

Swimming.

Trunks or commando? I thought to myself as I opened up the bottom drawer on my dresser and shifted through the various swimsuits I owned. Blue or red? Or perhaps green? Orange for the start of autumn?

As I contemplated my options, I heard the muffled ring of my cellphone. I had to search through my laundry hamper until I found it half-buried in the pocket of my sports jacket. An unknown number flashed across the screen. "Spam, probably," I said aloud, half ready to let it go to voicemail but for some reason, I got the weird feeling that I should answer. "Hello?"

"Cain?" The voice on the other end of the line sounded uncertain.

"Axel?" I guessed.

"Yes," he answered. "From the club last night."

"I was hoping you'd give me a call." A smile stretched across my lips as I sat down on the edge of the bed. "I just never thought it would come so soon."

"I'd like to have a word."

"You can have a word with me now."

"In person."

"This doesn't sound very promising." I was usually the kind of person who basked in their own confidence but right now I had a bubbling of doubt creeping along the length of my throat, threatening to choke me.

"It's nothing serious," he assured. "It's just that after last night, I'd like to see you again."

My shoulders sagged a few inches as relief washed over me. "Alright. Well, I plan on going for a dip. Would you mind joining me?"

"Where?"

"My backyard. I have a heated pool so make sure to bring some trunks." I pictured the football player wearing nothing but a flimsy swimsuit and it got my blood rushing. That blood concentrated right between my legs, erecting my boner to full mast in a matter of seconds.

"Send over your address and I'll be there."

"Will do," I breathed.

"See you soon." And with that, he clicked off the call. I couldn't believe it. I was about to have one of the most sought-after playboys over for a swim. This was going to be... interesting.

***

I was cooling off after a few laps when I heard the squeak of the back gate. And there he stood, looking even sexier in the midday sun. His skin was a stunning shade of toasted almond. He was the kind of man that simply soaked up the sun and turned it into the honey of his body.

"You look nice," I purred as soon as he took off his clothes and revealed some tight-fitting swim trunks.

He didn't say a single word as he climbed onto the diving board. With perfect form, he jumped toward the clouds and hovered there a moment. I had to squint against the brightness just to see the arch of his back as he dove toward the water and pierced the glass-like surface. I held my breath as I waited for him to reappear.

Suddenly, he grabbed my ankle and tugged me into the water. I opened my eyes and saw him through a haze of tinted blue. His hair danced around his head like a halo. I gravitated toward him but before I could close the distance between our bodies, he propelled himself to the surface and hoisted himself onto the side of the pool. "Nice place you got here," he said as he moved his feet through the water.

"I would call it modest compared to the mansion you must live in."

He shrugged. "Sometimes, less is more." He leaned back, propping himself up on his elbows.

I sat down beside him. "I have a feeling that there's more to this visit than just a friendly little swim."

He nodded, eyes pinched. "Last night was amazing – don't get me wrong. I'm sure you felt the chemistry between our bodies as much as I did but all the same, I can't help but feel wrong for feeling this attraction when you're my best friend's ex."

This felt like a slap to the face. Why lead me on if he only planned to crush me underneath his heel?

"So, why are you here?"

"Because I want to know what really happened between the two of you. Riley has never really opened up about it and I just want to know why he's still down in the dumps about it after all this time."

"Wait, he's still hung up about it?" I asked.

"Like you wouldn't believe."

I frowned. "But we broke up over a year ago."

"I know. I've told him its time to move on but he just keeps on wallowing. It can't be healthy."

I rubbed my hands against my knees. "If I'm totally honest, the breakup was my fault and it pains me to admit that. I was an asshole at the time. All the time, I was making good money as a stockbroker. So much so, that I didn't know what to do with it. I blew it on useless crap until I drove Riley away for the thrill of sleeping around. Big mistake. The thrill didn't last very long and soon I felt empty inside. There was no point in me going back to Riley since breaking up had broken his heart."

"You didn't sleep around while you were still together, did you?"

"No. I never cheated on Riley. I didn't even think of it. I only started sleeping around when we were separated."

"I see."

"I would love to make things right with him but I've never had the courage to apologize as I should."

"So, you want to get back together with Riley?"

"In many ways, yes."

Axel furrowed his brows together with confusion. "Then why did you insist on dancing with me? Riley was right there –"

"Because you're cute too," I interrupted. "And I couldn't help myself."

"No argument there," he chuckled.

Suddenly, this serious expression washed over him.

"What?"

"You might think me crazy but I've just had an idea and I think maybe, it's just wild enough to work."

# Chapter 5: Riley

That night.

The smell of sizzling hamburger meat wafted through the air. It wasn't gourmet by any means but sometimes, a guy just wants a good 'ol burger.

Missy jumped, trying to snag the patty off the grill.

"No!" I blocked her with my body to keep her from burning herself. "Bad girl."

Her tail dropped between her legs. Feeling bad for yelling at her, I picked up one of her toys and threw it across the yard. She immediately bounded after it giving me the space I needed to finish cooking. I flipped over the patty and saw a bit of charcoal around the edges.

Perfect, I thought as I slid it onto a hamburger bun. I turned around to grab the condiments and that's when I saw them. I nearly jumped right out of my skin. My spatula fell onto the grass.

"How long have you two been standing there?" I gasped. "And who invited you here, anyway?" I narrowed my eyes at Cain. My heart still throbbed for my ex despite everything he had done. Most nights, I still wanted to turn back the clock and relive that magical time we spent together.

Axel stepped forward. "No need to start off with hostilities. We come here waving the white flag of truce."

"What the hell are you talking about?"

Missy ran forward, jumping on Axel. As that happened, Cain revealed a great big bouquet of flowers. Okay, this was getting weirder and weirder.

Cain held them out for me to grab.

I hesitated.

"I don't understand what's going on. Why are you two here – together."

"It's high time I apologize for what I did," Cain started. "I was a major asshole and I know it. I've had to live with the repercussions of leaving you – of feeling this hollowness in my chest when I'm forced to sleep without your warmth."

His words were everything I had ever wanted to hear. "But..." I glanced over at Axel. "I'm still a little confused." Still, I took the flowers and sniffed them. They were autumn blooms and some of my favorites too. I was surprised that Cain remembered my love for mums.

Axel managed to get Missy to leave him alone by feeding her my dinner. I wanted to protest but there was such strange energy buzzing between the three of us that my tongue felt like sandpaper.

"Cain was a little shy about apologizing so I said I would tag along for moral support, you know?"

I thought it was a little odd but I didn't question it. There was something odd going on but I couldn't quite put my finger on it. Plus, it didn't help that Axel was looking at me like a butcher looking at a prime cut of meat. He was starting to freak me out. Was there something on my face that I didn't know about?

Feeling a little self-conscious, I shifted from foot to foot.

"I know that I treated you poorly." Cain's voice broke my train of thought. I turned my head in his direction and our eyes locked together. His gaze was enough to bring back a stream of old memories. I had been at my happiest when I was by his side. My palm itched, remembering the way his hand had felt against mine.

Right.

"And I've learned to be better than that."

"So, what are you asking for, a second chance?" My voice didn't sound like my own as I asked the question.

"Sort of."

"Sort of?" I raised my eyebrow. "What does that mean, sort of?"

Cain looked over at Axel who took a step forward, positioning himself between the two of us. "If you want an exclusive relationship with Cain, then that's fine. I won't get in the way."

Wait, what?

"But I'm putting a new offer on the table."

"What are you talking about?" I blurted, head spinning with a million and one different interpretations.

Did he mean...? No. Axel's never been interested – or, has he?

"A threesome."

The words fell from his lips like a boulder.

"A threesome?" I repeated, dumbfounded. "You mean...?" I pointed at all three of us a couple of times, painting myself as a complete idiot who didn't know what to do with his hands. "Us?"

"Yes, us," Axel answered as if it were the most normal thing in the world to have a threesome with both your best friend and your ex-boyfriend.

Am I dreaming or something? I pinched myself just to make sure.

Pain.

Okay, I'm awake. But this is fucking insane. My brain couldn't even start to make sense of his offer. "You mean like a threesome, threesome?" I made some weird gesture with my hand as if that would clarify things.

"I don't know what you mean by that but yes, a threesome. You know, where all three of us get under the sheets and rock the bed until morning."

I couldn't believe how nonchalant Axel was when suggesting such a situation. "I..."

"If you don't want to, that's okay." Cain rested a hand on my shoulder.

"On one condition."

"Which is?" Axel asked as he looked me right in the eye. That piercing gaze of his cut right through me. Now I knew why he was considered the playboy of the century. Axel was fucking hot. Why hadn't

I noticed it before? I'd be a damned fool to let this opportunity slip me by. But, at the same time, I wasn't prepared for a casual relationship. If they wanted me then they had to prove it.

"I want the two of you to stop sleeping around."

"So, you want an exclusive threesome relationship?" Cain asked.

"Yes. If we're going to do this then I want us to be committed to one another."

"No sleeping around at all?" This time it was Axel who asked the question. "I'd be stuck with you two?"

I recoiled. His words felt like an insult until he flashed a smile.

"Looks like I'm one lucky man."

"What?" I sputtered.

"I said, I'm one lucky man." His smile deepened. "Especially if it means I get to have you both any time I'd like."

"I wouldn't say any time –"

But Axel already had me by the hair. His lips collided with mine. I never thought that kissing my best friend could be such a soul-lifting experience but trust me, it was. As the kiss intensified, I felt weightless. My brain still ran through all the flaws with this little plan of his but my heart told me to roll with it. This was what I wanted and it was time I stopped running.

He pulled away. "So, is that a yes?"

"Yes..." I mumbled. "Hell yes."

Cain and I exchanged a knowing glance. "Well, in that case, why don't we share our first dinner together?" Cain made his way toward the grill but before he could make it very far, Axel grabbed him by the wrist and reeled him back so he was pinned against the football player's muscular chest.

"Dinner?" he said. "I think I would rather have dessert first." I knew as soon as Axel used that deep, husky voice of his, neither one of us stood a chance. "And I'm not taking no for an answer."

Before I could react, he pushed me down onto one of the lawn chairs. He was about to start ripping off my clothing but Missy bounded over, thinking we were playing some kind of game.

Cain tried to hold her back but she was insistent on licking Axel's face.

"If we want some privacy, might I suggest we bring this inside?" My cock was throbbing against the fabric of my pants and I really couldn't wait any longer. I needed these men just as much as I needed air to breathe.

Axel swept me off my feet and carried me through the sliding doors. Cain was in charge of closing them and keeping Missy outside. She looked distraught at first but upon discovering one of her toys, she quickly forgot about us.

"Now, where were we?" He tossed me onto the couch.

"Are you sure you don't want to take this to the bedroom?" I asked.

"Too far," he growled as his lips traveled along the side of my neck. "I want you now."

My shirt was the first article to go. It flew across the room and landed on the coffee table. Then came the button to my pants. It dinged against the window.

"Careful!" Cain protested as he ducked to avoid getting hit in the face with my jeans.

Axel smirked. "What do we have here?" he asked as he grabbed my package through my boxer briefs. I gasped and arched my back as his grip tightened.

"Don't you dare start teasing me," I whispered, my breath already ragged.

"Oh?" he mused. "And what are you going to do about it, Riley? I have you exactly where I want you and from this point forward, you're just my helpless little plaything." Axel was such an alpha that it had me reeling. My whole body quivered with the need to surrender to his strength.

He was right.

Assured of this fact, Axel went back to kissing my neck. This time, his teeth nipped against the skin, leaving behind faint love bites.

I moaned, hips bucking into the air to meet his.

Damn, I thought. He feels huge and that's the goddamn understatement of the year right there.

# Chapter 6: Axel

Seeing Riley with his back arched, body yearning for mine, had me seeing him in a whole new light.

Mmm, and what a delicious light it is, I thought as I slipped my hands underneath his body and cupped his ass cheeks. They were nice and firm – exactly what I liked. I gave them a nice squeeze.

He moaned, head thrown back with the pleasure.

I can't believe it took me this long to fuck this man.

"Someone's excited," I whispered as I once again took his package in my hand. This time, the boxers were off and I got to feel every inch of his smooth skin against my palm. He was the kind of guy that kept himself cleanly shaven.

Good.

Because that would make him nice and sensitive and I liked the guys who made a lot of noise.

I sunk to my knees and pushed his legs apart. When that wasn't enough, I slung them over my shoulder.

"Relax." I rubbed the inside of his thighs. "There's nothing for you to be nervous about. Just lean back and enjoy the ride."

As I spoke, my hands got closer and closer to his balls until finally, I took hold of them. They rolled between my fingers.

"Axel..."

"What's the matter?" I asked as if I was the most innocent man in the world. "Is something wrong?"

"Please..." There was a fire burning in his eyes and I suppose it was cruel of me to tease him like this but I just couldn't help myself. I wanted to take him to the very brink of insanity. I wanted him to know that Cain and I were the only two men on this planet that could make him feel this good.

He rolled his head back and that's when I made my move. I leaned forward ever so slightly until I was sure he could feel my warm breath against his length. It hardened in response. I chuckled as it twitched. "Oh, someone wants me really bad, huh?" My tongue traced along his underside all the way up to his tip. There, I swirled it around.

Riley bucked his hips into the air, forcing me to hold him down.

Our eyes locked.

I answered him with a dirty little grin before I wrapped my lips around his girth. Without an ounce of hesitation, I started to bob my head up and down, gaining some momentum.

Already, I could feel the throbbing of his cock. I didn't want him to blow just yet so when his toes curled, I stopped.

He whimpered, eyes wide. "Why?"

"Come now, Riley, I didn't think you were the selfish type." I waved my arm over at Cain who was having a grand 'ol time beating it off at the sight of us. "It wouldn't be very fair of us if we excluded Cain, now would it?"

Cain looked up and locked eyes with his ex-lover.

"Go on then, make up for lost time." I winked.

Riley was still in too much of a daze to move. But Cain was quick to act on the offer. He pounced on his lover and pinned him to the couch. While they ate face with one another, I slipped off into the bedroom and rummaged through some of his drawers. Just as I had expected – lube – and the good kind too.

When I returned to the living room, the two of them were deep in a sixty-nine. It was one hell of a sight. Riley was choking on Cain's dick and yet, he grabbed at the stock broker's ass like he never wanted to breathe again. Cain, on the other hand, was having more than his fair share of fun running his tongue around and around the base of Riley's balls. I could tell by the way he gyrated his hips with frustration that he was coming close to his breaking point.

I cleared my throat. Cain looked up. I threw him the bottle of lube. His whole face lit up.

"Bend over the couch but don't you stop sucking his cock," I ordered.

Cain was quick to obey. Once he was in position, I took my place behind his ass. It was a bit more supple than Riley's but still a hell of a sight to look at. Given the chance, I wouldn't have minded looking at it all day long.

The thought turned me on even more than I already was. My cock was dying for release but I held back the desire to pounce on these men. This was our first time together and I wanted it to last.

I lubed up my fingers and slowly introduced them to Cain's asshole. He fought against me at first but with a little persistence on my part, he started to open up. First, it was my middle finger. I twisted it nice and slow. "That's it," I cooed against his ear. "Take it all." My finger penetrated him down to the very last knuckle.

He moaned against Riley's cock which just sent Riley into a frenzy. He jerked, right on the brink of orgasm.

"Stop." I pulled on Cain's hair, yanking him off of Riley's rock-hard member.

They both looked at me like they had been utterly betrayed.

"Did you really think I'd let you cum that early on in the game?" The corner of my lip twitched with amusement. "Now, I suggest you get down on your knees." I snapped and Riley was right there where I wanted him to be.

His mouth was hotter than I expected it to be. And his lips – pure silk. It was hard for me to concentrate when he had a way of bobbing his head. My legs turned to jelly. I could barely stand. Still, I held my ground as I added another finger to Cain's asshole, stretching him out. Better this way than him getting ripped apart by my monster cock.

"Fuck," I growled. Somehow, Riley had me deep throated. My cock kept ramming down his throat but he didn't even seem to mind. And then when he started fondling my balls, I could barely take it.

Knowing I would blow at any second, I pushed Cain onto the couch and pulled his ass into the air, watching as he swayed it from side to side like a little nymph trying to entice me.

Without much warning, I rammed my length into his waiting hole. To make things easier on him, I added a bit more lube to the mix so he was nice and slippery. Growing sex crazed, I grabbed him by the hair and fucked him like a wild bronco.

Riley took his natural place at Cain's head, forcing his mouth up and down his length.

The sight only added to my excitement. I grabbed Cain by the hips and rammed into him harder and harder. I didn't want to stop even as my balls tightened. I was so close to the edge that I could feel it underneath my feet. Still, I fucked him like a piston – in and out – in and out.

I grabbed his cock and stroked it, waiting for him to blow. I didn't think it would take very long. He was already dripping with precum and when my thumb started to run along his tip, he went absolutely nuts.

Even as I held him by the shoulders, he jerked like a madman.

Riley screamed and pulled out his cock just in time to shoot it all over Cain's face. It was quite the mess.

Cain looked shocked by the amount of jizz but that wasn't reason enough for me to stop. In fact, it led me to fuck him even harder. I swear the whole couch was threatening to collapse as I lost all control.

I snarled and tore at his skin, leaving red marks all down the length of his back. My hand moved at a fierce rhythm, determined to make him climax before I did.

Cain howled with pleasure and a second later, his hot, sticky cum was all over the place.

Riley was right there to clean up the last few drops from his tip. "Mmm," he said with a toothy smile. "I haven't had something that sweet in a long time."

Cain was panting for breath. I continued my assault until a wave of pleasure overtook me. My whole body went rigid and my toes curled against the couch. A hiss escaped from between my teeth as my cock exploded with the moment.

Ah, my mind went blank as string after string of cum shot from my tip and deep inside my newfound lover.

Spent of the rest of my energy, I collapsed on top of him.

Riley appeared with a wet washcloth and cleaned off his ex's face. He was gentle about it and even finished the job with a little kiss to the tip of his nose.

"That was amazing," I breathed when no one dared to break the silence that had settled all around us.

"Amazing?" Riley repeated. "That doesn't even come close to describing it." He sat on the other side of me and rested his head on my shoulder. I wrapped my arm around his shoulders and pulled him a little closer. "That was absolutely mind-blowing."

"Tell me about it," Cain chimed in. "I never pegged myself as someone who would like a threesome so damn much."

"Me neither," Riley agreed. "That was one hell of an idea, Axel."

I smiled. "What can I say? I'm a genius."

Riley rolled his eyes. "I see that modesty is still something you lack."

"Lack?" I cocked my head to the side. "Who needs modesty when you're nothing but skill." My hand fell to his thigh. "Do you think I could have you screaming with modesty?"

He blushed.

"What now?" Cain asked. "I feel like I can't move a single muscle. You two will just have to carry me everywhere."

"I think that can be arranged." Even though my legs still felt like jelly, I managed to get up and carry Cain into the bedroom. While I placed him down on the mattress, I heard Riley open up the back door, letting Missy back inside.

He had a hard time keeping her from the bedroom but by some miracle, he managed to close the door.

"I'm thinking we all take a nice, warm bath," Riley suggested. "Or we're going to get really sticky, really fast."

"No arguing there," I said as I picked up Cain one more time.

"I could get used to this," he grinned as he wrapped his arms around my neck.

Riley ran the hot water while I placed Cain down on the sink. Since I had time to waste, I brought him into a kiss. His lips weren't quite as sweet as Riley's but they were definitely a close second.

I savored the taste even as I bit down on his bottom lip and gave it a little tug.

He moaned slightly and even though we had just finished our lovemaking, his cock still gave a twitch of excitement.

I chuckled and ran my hand down his length. "Don't," he begged.

"Alright, alright," I conceded. I loved teasing my partners but I didn't want to come across as being unusually cruel. I knew how sensitive his cock must have felt. "I'll play nice."

Riley sunk into the water, half submerged under a thick layer of bubbles.

"Seriously?" I asked. "What are we? A bunch of five-year-olds?"

"You're never too old for a bubble bath," he countered. "And, if you don't want to join me, that's your problem. More space for Cain and me."

Cain jumped down from the sink and joined my best friend.

"I thought you couldn't walk."

"Well, I saw something I just couldn't resist," he answered with a sly grin. "Now quit bitching and come join us, will you?"

"Be careful what you ask for."

# Chapter 7: Riley

The following morning.

I tried to turn to the other side of my bed but there was something extremely warm blocking my way. I opened my eyes and blinked against the brightness filtering through the curtains. My vision was still blurry when a big, strong arm wrapped itself around my chest and tightened into a bear grip. I could barely breathe.

"Let... go..." I wheezed through gritted teeth.

Then another arm was draped over top of me, making my situation even worse.

Bark!

The two men jerked to a seated position, eyes wide.

We locked eyes.

"So, that wasn't a dream..." I whispered to myself. "We actually did it."

"You mean, we did each other," Axel said with a wink.

Cain giggled. "I still can't believe it myself." As he spoke, he ran his fingertips along my naked chest. Oh, it felt so good to feel his touch. My heart skipped a beat at the familiarity of it.

"Mmm, your touch is still as magical as I remember..." I purred as I nuzzled my head into his neck.

Axel cuddled up against me and I immediately felt the hardness of his member settle between my ass cheeks. I gasped and tried to pull away but he reeled me even closer. "Where do you think you're going?" he growled against my ear. "You're staying right here."

His cock gave a twitch of excitement.

Am I the one turning him on or is this just his morning wood?

"This is nice," he murmured against my ear as he took hold of my lobe and tugged on it.

Goosebumps prickled my skin, gathering at the back of my neck. This was everything I had ever wanted and yet, there was this tightness in my chest. Was I doing the right thing? Or would everything crash and burn?

"I need to get up," I said. "Some of us have to go to work."

This time, it was Cain who cuddled into me. "Five more minutes."

"Seriously, what time is it?" I was starting to get anxious. Some people might call me anal retentive but I just like things to be organized and punctuality is sort of my thing. In my five years of employment, I had yet to miss a shift. I wasn't about to start.

"Calm down," Axel held me a little tighter.

"Guys, I'm not playing around."

Axel sighed. "Fine. Scurry off. We'll catch up with you in the kitchen."

I managed to untangle myself from the mess of limbs. There was a slight aching in my loins as I walked toward the bathroom. There, I locked the door. In the mirror, my reflection looked a little brighter than normal.

Did last night make me happy? I asked myself. I don't know.

***

The kitchen was quiet but still, I wasn't able to think. My mind was buzzing like a swarm of bees.

What do I do? Do I run along with this or do I nip it in the bud before it becomes any more serious?

Even the black cup of coffee I was drinking churned inside my stomach. I poured it down the drain and tried to clear my mind from the clutter of doubt.

Missy walked in with one of her toys in her mouth. She dropped it by my feet, tail wagging. "Wow, you're actually letting me take this without making a fuss over it?" I waved it back and forth. Her head moved to follow its path. "Do you want it girl, do you?" She jumped up in response to my high-pitched voice. Before she could tackle me to the ground, I threw the toy into the living room. Seeing as it would be too much trouble to bring it back, she laid it down and started chewing on it, looking for an opening to the stuffing. "If only my life were as easy as yours. I'd have nothing to worry about other than chew toys and begging for treats."

I slumped into a nearby kitchen chair and browsed my phone, trying to kill the few extra minutes I had before I needed to leave. Upstairs, I heard laughter. They were probably better off without me.

Maybe they're just including you as an act of pity, came that little voice at the back of my head. Maybe they feel sorry for you.

My lack of self-confidence made me feel like absolute shit. A heaviness settled on my shoulders, making them sag. Was it true? I wondered.

Unable to stand their laughter any longer, I grabbed my jacket and my laptop bag. As I slung it over my shoulder, I hesitated. I was playing with fire by agreeing to this. Not only had a slept with someone who had broken my heart once before but there was a very real possibility that I could lose my best friend. I blinked away the thought because losing Axel just wasn't something I wanted to think about.

Ring! Ring!

The suddenness of my ringtone blaring against the otherwise quiet home nearly had me jumping out of my skin. With shaking fingers, I managed to fish my phone out of my pocket and answer it. "H-Hello?" My voice cracked. This whole thing was definitely getting to me.

Get a grip, man, came that little voice. Great, one more person to taunt me.

"Riley. I'm glad I caught you. I know you'll be at the office soon but I need you to go down to the lake right away."

It was my boss' monotone voice. I would have recognized it just about anywhere.

"What's going on?" I asked.

"There's been a problem."

"What kind of problem?"

"Look, I don't have time to explain right now. I just need you down there as quick as you can."

Click.

Before I could ask anything else, he had already hung up the call.

Weird, I thought. Something must be seriously wrong for him to be this worked up. He never calls me on my personal cell phone number.

I reached forward and grabbed the doorknob but something had me turning around. I marched back into the kitchen and scribbled a note telling the guys where I was. Then I grabbed Missy's leash and off we went.

***

At the lake, I met up with my boss who was busy yelling into the receiver of his phone. I didn't need him to provide me with an explanation. The problem was clear as could be.

A large pipe on the other side of the lake was pouring out dark-colored sludge and it was contaminating the entire body of water. Already, there were hundreds of fishes belly up on the surface.

"What do they think they're doing?" I asked aloud. "This is protected land."

"It's that new factory. The town gave them some tax breaks in exchange for a new load of jobs for the unemployed but now they think they own this place."

"How long has this been going on for?"

"A few hours or so."

"And it's already this bad?"

"That stuff is toxic."

I cursed under my breath. This was bad. Really bad. "We have to stop them. Have you tried talking to them?"

"I've asked the authorities to come have a look but they claim they're 'busy,' as always."

"Typical. They don't want to help us." I huffed. "Well, if they don't want to do it then I'll just do it myself."

"You can't."

"What's going to stop me? This lake means the world to me. I'm not going to let someone destroy it for their capital greed."

"This is a mistake –" He was about to say something more but his phone started to ring. He took the call and it gave me the perfect opportunity to make my getaway.

***

Talking with the factory wasn't as easy as I thought it would be. They called the cops about five minutes after I started shouting my threats. Probably not my brightest moment.

"You can't do this!" I protested as the officers tried to get me into the back of their police cruiser. "You don't understand what you're doing. This is an infringement on my freedom of speech not to mention the integrity of our wildlife. If they keep this up, they are going to put species on the endangered list –"

"Get rid of him, please." The corporate head had no emotion to his voice.

"What about my dog?"

But no one cared as they slammed the door in my face.

"And did you have to make these handcuffs so damned uncomfortable?"

The two police officers exchanged a silent glance but they didn't bother to comment. Apparently, I wasn't worth their time.

***

Down at the station, I was given one call to try and get me out of this mess. I thought about calling my boss but given the situation, the line would probably be busy. So, that left me with one choice: Axel.

I whispered a silent prayer as I dialed his number. It was one of the only numbers I knew by heart.

The dial tone was obnoxiously loud against my ear. I held my breath, chest tightening with the lack of air.

Please pick up. Please, Axel. Don't let me down. These words kept repeating over and over again in my head. I need you.

"I'm sorry but the number you have dialed cannot be answered –"

I dropped the phone at the sound of the operator. My heart felt like it had fallen straight down to my feet. Every inch of my body had turned to ice. "No..." I whispered.

"Come on," an officer probed. "You had your call –"

"No, you don't understand. There has to be some kind of mistake –"

"No mistake," he said, voice stern. "Now, you'd better get in the holding cell before you regret it."

I gulped, eyes gravitating toward the nightstick hanging at his hip.

With my feet feeling like they were made out of lead, I followed him down a narrow hall. He opened up a metal door and shoved me into a cell full of scary-looking people. Every single one of them gave me the stink eye. Keeping my head down, I shuffled over to a corner and kept to myself.

How am I going to get out of this one?

# Chapter 8: Cain

I must have fallen asleep because when I next opened my eyes, Riley was gone and Axel was snoring. I smiled. Who would have thought that I would end up sleeping with both my ex-boyfriend and a super-hot football player? Had I won the relationship jackpot or something?

Drawn in by the man's warmth, I shimmied closer, taking Riley's now empty spot.

"Mmm," Axel mused as he held me tight against his chest. He had quite the grip.

"Let's not break my back first thing in the morning," I said.

"Hmm?"

"Are you awake?" I asked but all I got was another mumbled response. Seeing that it was hopeless to wake the slumbering quarterback, I rolled out of bed and searched for my clothing. I like lounging around commando as much as the next guy but Riley's house was a little on the chilly side. Seriously, my nipples were rock hard. I tried to warm them but they still poked through my shirt as soon as I put it on.

My pants were shoved underneath the couch. How they had managed to get there was beyond my level of understanding.

"What a sight," purred Axel. I hadn't even heard him walk into the room. He slapped my ass, making me jump. Before I could regain my bearings, he was on top of me, lips smashed against mine.

My eyes widened with surprise before I melted against the show of intimacy. As his tongue swept into my mouth, my heart thudded with the crazy beat of passion. My hands fell to his lower back as my hands traced invisible patterns all over his skin.

"Mmm, that feels good," he whispered against my ear. The hotness of his breath had my body reeling with desire. All I wanted to do was push him against the couch and have my way with him. But it almost felt wrong to do that when Riley wasn't around. "What's wrong?" Axel asked, picking up on my apprehension.

"Where do you think Riley ran off to?"

"Work, probably."

"But it's a Saturday," I said.

"Doesn't matter. That guy will go to work on Christmas if it means impressing his boss –" Suddenly, Axel's face drained of color. It legitimately looked like he had just seen a ghost.

"What?"

"Is the time on the clock correct?" he asked, pointing at an analog clock Riley had hanging on the wall.

"I don't see why not." Just to make sure, I checked my wrist. Somehow, it had survived the wild events of last night. "Yeah, that's right."

"Shit, shit, shit." A slew of swear words erupted from Axel's lips. "I'm going to be late and the couch is going to skin me alive!" Naked, he started running for the bedroom, cock swinging from side to side. Man, what a sight to behold. A second later, he returned, cock still swinging. "Where are my clothes?"

"What's the emergency?"

"What's the emergency?" he repeated like I had just slapped him right in the face. "The emergency is that I'm going to be late for practice and we need all the practice we can get this season."

In his frantic state, he walked right past his pants. I had to hand them over to him. "So, you're going to practice in jeans?"

"No, of course not. I have a change of clothes in the locker room but I can't exactly show up on the field buck naked."

"I think I would pay to see that," I said with a chuckle. "And so would most of the world."

"Very funny." He snatched his shirt from my hand and tossed it on.

"Do you think I could go with you?"

"Go with me?" He tilted his head to the side. "Why?"

"I just want to see my new boyfriend doing what he does best." I batted my eyelashes to sweeten the deal. "I swear, you won't even know I'm there."

"I don't suppose it'll be a problem," he said. "But we're leaving now."

"Right."

"But where in fuck's name are my keys?"

"Have you tried your pocket?" I suggested.

He reached inside and there they were.

"I had no idea you were so scatterbrained."

"Now's not the time, Cain," he growled before taking me by the wrist and towing me through the front door.

"Should we lock this –"

"No time."

He practically pushed me into the passenger seat.

"You're acting like you're late to the Superbowl," I said as I buckled myself into place. "It's just practice. Can't you ease up a bit?"

Axel shot me a deadly glare. "No, I can't ease up a bit. I've failed to bring my team to victory in the past and this is my final shot. If I fuck this up then the coach is going to replace me with a rookie and I'm not going to let that happen. This year, I'm going to show him that I mean business."

I couldn't argue with the pure determination in his voice. Nor could I find the voice to speak when Axel was driving like a madman. I kept flinching as he narrowly squeezed through spaces in traffic that no sane person would ever attempt.

"Maybe you should slow down..." I was clutching my seat for dear life.

Honk!

Axel forced someone to swerve out of the way and he didn't even break a sweat doing it.

"Is this normal for you?"

No answer.

"Alright... I guess I'll just watch my life flash before my eyes over here."

***

Somehow, we made it to the stadium in one piece. Adrenaline was still coursing through my veins by the time I took a seat on the bleachers. It was strange to see some of my favorite players out in the open like this. They were all mind-bogglingly massive.

One of the defensemen came jogging in my direction. He grabbed a water bottle from the cooler right in front of me. "Are you the new water boy?" he asked.

"No. I'm..." I trailed off, not quite sure how I should introduce myself.

"He's my boyfriend," Axel interjected.

The defenseman shook his head. "Another one? Why don't you just stick to girls like the rest of us?"

"Because, unlike you, I can sleep with anyone – and I mean anyone."

A flair of jealousy sparked through my chest. He was speaking the truth. Someone with Axel's money, fame, and good looks could slip under the sheets with just about anyone which meant that Riley and I could get thrown aside faster than it takes to blink.

The defenseman looked me over and huffed. "I've had better."

"Don't listen to him." Axel placed a hand on my shoulder as soon as his teammate had walked away. "He's just trying to get inside my head."

"Does he not like you?"

"You could say that."

"Why?"

"Because I'm the quarterback. He's one of the best players in the league but no matter what he does, everyone's still looking at me."

"I see..."

"Hey, is everything okay?" He squeezed my shoulder. "You look worried about something."

"No, it's nothing," I answered. "Don't sweat it."

A whistle was blown and Axel excused himself to join his team. I watched, my arms wrapped around my torso as a sudden chill penetrated through to my bones. Why would Axel settle for a couple of normal guys when he had the option of doing so much better? What did we have to offer him that others didn't?

I bit my bottom lip to keep my doubt from mounting.

What if he gets bored of us?

Now, I'm not usually the self-conscious type but when you're dating footballs #1 playboy, it's kind of hard not to be. Nearly every female and gay guy in America had their eyes set on the hunk and that wasn't something I particularly enjoyed.

These thoughts were pushed away as soon as the field came into motion. I kept my eyes locked on the prize. Axel was certainly in his element. He had an undeniable control over his team. They were like malleable metal that Axel bent at his will.

Seeing him, my attraction for the man only heightened. Just when I thought he couldn't get any hotter – I saw him throwing a football. Every time the ball flew off his fingertips his body would tighten into a deep coil, spine twisted. It accentuated the taper of his waist and the broadness of his shoulders. This guy was nothing less than a Greek God and somehow, he was all mine – well, almost – I was willing to share with Riley.

Halfway through the routine, he returned to the bleachers, all hot and sweaty.

"Enjoying the show?" he asked.

"Like you wouldn't even believe."

***

"So, what do you think your chances are this year?" I asked once we were back in the car together.

"I'm feeling pretty good about it," he said as he rested his hand on my thigh. He kept it there even as he cruised along the backroads. I was glad that he had stopped driving like a damned maniac. Now, this? This was something I could enjoy. I rolled down my window and caught the scent of a faraway bonfire.

"I love that smell."

"What smell?" His nostrils twitched as he tried to pick up that classic late-summer smell.

"Oh, a fire, huh?" He smiled. "You know, it's been a while since I got to make some smores. My dietician isn't going to be happy if he finds out but I think my secret is safe with you."

I zipped my lips and grinned.

"That's what I thought."

"Shouldn't we pick up Riley. Surely, he's home from work, right?"

Axel nodded. "Yeah, probably. It's already pretty late and I can't really see him working overtime on a Saturday. And, if he was, I'd assume he'd shoot us a text or something."

"Right," I agreed.

We pulled up to his driveway but from what I could tell, all the lights were still off.

"Weird," Axel said as he got out of the car. He tried the door and it was still unlocked. "Guess he's not home yet."

I wandered toward the kitchen thinking that would be the most likely place to find him since it was almost dinner time and he had an obsession with cooking but all I found was an empty coffee mug in the sink.

Then, I found a note. It had blended in with the whiteness of the countertops. I picked it up but before I could read a single word, there came a knock at the front door. I dropped the note back to where it was before and joined Axel at the door.

There stood a woman holding Missy by the leash. Her eyes nearly bugged straight out of her head when she recognized Axel. "Wait..." she stammered. "Aren't you?"

Axel flashed her a charming smile.

Again, that feeling of jealousy flashed inside my chest. My teeth mashed together as I tried to hold back the feeling of uncertainty. Axel wouldn't just abandon us for some random chick. Maybe the threesome was just lust-based but deep down, I knew there was more to it than that – there had to be.

"Where did you find that dog?" Axel was the first to break the silence.

"Oh?" The woman looked down and seemed surprised that there was a dog standing right beside her. "I found her wandering around the woods. The tag said to bring her here. Are you her owner?"

"No. She belongs to my best friend." Axel took the leash and I watched as his fingertips brushed against the back of her hand.

Is he doing this on purpose or am I just letting the jealousy get to my head? I asked myself.

"Thank you."

The girl blushed. "Do you think that maybe I could get your autograph or something? My boyfriend is totally going to lose his mind when he finds out that I got to meet you in person."

Relief washed over me. Okay, she's taken. She's not gunning to steal one of your boyfriends, I reassured myself.

"Sure thing." Axel disappeared to find a sharpie while I was left to awkwardly stand there with one of his fans. Luckily, he didn't take too long. "What would you like me to sign?"

"Um, my shoe, I guess." She wore white Converses and they were the perfect canvas for what she wanted.

"There you go!"

"Thank you so much!"

"Don't mention it." Axel flashed another smile and I swear the girl melted straight to the floor. He closed the door and turned to look in my direction. "That was weird."

"Did you have to flirt with her?" The question blurted out of my mouth before I could find the willpower to stop myself.

"Flirt with her?" he questioned. "What are you talking about? I wasn't flirting with anyone."

"Didn't look that way to me."

He reached forward and cupped my cheek against his palm. "Don't tell me you're jealous."

I looked away, unable to make eye contact with the football player.

"Cain." He placed two fingers underneath my chin and lifted it slightly so I was forced to look at his face. "You have nothing to worry about. I'm not going anywhere."

Silence settled between us until Missy whimpered and pawed at the door like she wanted to get out.

"Where is Riley?" Axel asked aloud. "He wouldn't leave Missy all by herself."

"Do you think...?" I didn't need to finish the question because I could feel that deep foreboding sensation at the pit of my stomach. "Something is wrong."

# Chapter 9: Axel

"There's a note in the kitchen but I haven't read it yet," Cain said as he walked in that direction. He picked it up and held it to the light so he could better read Riley's handwriting.

"What does it say?" I asked. There was a heaviness in the air that made me worry. Had something happened to my best friend?

"It says that there was some kind of emergency at the lake and that he was called in to check it out."

"That's it?"

"That's it," he confirmed. "Doesn't say when he's coming back. Doesn't say much of anything." He turned over the sheet of paper but it was blank. "Maybe we should give him a call."

I nodded in agreement and dialed his number. As I waited for him to pick up, I found myself pacing around the kitchen table like a caged animal trying to find a way to escape. Now, I've had my fair share of relationships in the past but my friendship with Riley had always been something special. He actually meant something to me and I never wanted to lose that.

"No answer," I said, the heaviness in the air thickening. It was becoming hard to breathe.

"I'm sure he's fine. Maybe his phone just died." Although Cain was trying to help the situation, his words did not comfort me. Already, my mind was racing with a million and one different scenarios.

"No," I said. "It's more than that." Thinking on my feet, I walked over to the side of the fridge where I found a magnet with his employer's contact information. "Bingo." I snatched it up and dialed the main line.

"Hello," came the voice of a female secretary. "You've reached Lakeside Micro; how may I help you?"

"I need to talk to Riley."

Silence.

I really did not like the sound of that.

"One moment please."

Before I could say a single word, I was placed on hold.

"What's going on?" Cain's whole face was painted with worry. It was good to know that he was just as invested in Riley's wellbeing as I was. Maybe they were exes but it was clear that they still cared for each other. Sometimes, people just need a second chance.

"I don't know yet. They have me listening to elevator music –"

"Hello?" This time, it was a male's voice.

"Hello, who is this?"

"Mr. Davit," he answered. "I heard you wanted to speak with Riley."

"Yes, this is his boyfriend."

"Boyfriend?" The man sounded shocked.

"Look, now is not the time for you to share that you're not fond of our type –"

"I wasn't implying that at all," he sputtered much too quickly. "I have nothing against men of... your nature."

I rolled my eyes. I really did not have the patience for this sort of thing, especially now. "Look, I just want to know what happened to Riley."

"Let me transfer –"

"Don't you dare."

But it was already too late. Again, the incessant elevator music started playing against my ear. I was really damn close to throwing the phone across the room.

"What's going on ¬–"

Before Cain could finish asking his question, there came a click through the line. "I swear, if I get put on hold one more time, there's going to be a problem."

"Relax, buster, no one is going to put you on hold." It was a familiar voice.

"Meg?"

"The one and only."

"Man am I glad to hear your voice," I said. "What's going on over there? Does no one know how to answer a simple question? Where's Riley?"

"He got arrested."

"Arrested?" I repeated. "What are you talking about?"

That was the thing about Meg, she was always straight with you. That was one of the reasons why I had liked her so much but, in the end, she couldn't keep up with my lifestyle and I didn't care enough to slow down for hers. Despite this, we broke it off on relatively good terms. If we hadn't, I doubt she'd be so willing to help me right now.

"The new factory in town has started pouring their sludge into the lake. Riley didn't take to it and decided he was going to give them a piece of his mind."

"The idiot," I mumbled underneath my breath. "What did he think he was going to accomplish on his own?"

"Apparently my boss said he was pretty adamant about it."

"Of course. Riley would die on a cross for that lake."

"Well, luckily there's only one jailhouse in town. I don't think it should be too hard to find your boyfriend."

"Thanks, Meg, I owe you one."

"I'll remember that." I could almost see her winking as I hung up the call. "We have to go," I said before Cain could even open up his mouth. "Now."

***

Being a football player comes with its perks – one of them being money. Just one of my bank accounts holds more money than most people ever make in a lifetime. So, suffice to say, I didn't have much trouble paying Riley's bond.

"Just sign here and your friend will be free to go."

I did as I was told.

"That was a ridiculous amount of money given that Riley did nothing more than trespassing," Cain commented as we waited for the guard to return.

"If I had to guess, this factory has been dishing out bribes."

"I wouldn't be surprised," Cain agreed. "Companies do it all the time to get where they need to go."

I shook my head. "Makes me sick –"

Just then, I spotted Riley. I couldn't help myself as I rushed forward and trapped him in a bear hug. "You're going to tell me everything."

He shook his head. "Not now, Axel. I just want to go home. This is not a day I soon want to repeat."

Seeing his fatigue, I agreed.

# Chapter 10: Riley

A few weeks later.

"When are they going to finish those letters?" I refreshed my email for the millionth time but still, it was empty. "I'm starting to get worried."

"Don't worry about it," Cain wrapped his arms around me while his lips traveled along the side of my neck. "They'll get it done."

I shove him off. "But each day that goes by, we're putting the lake in danger and if we lose that precious ecosystem, I don't even want to think about the repercussions."

"Would you relax?" Axel spoke up this time. He had the most nonchalant expression on his face as if nothing were amiss with the world. "I hired the best lawyers in town. They are doing everything they can to try and remedy this situation."

"I fail to see that." I was starting to get all worked up. "It's been nearly a month and no one seems to care –"

"Everyone cares but these things take time," Cain took my wrist and pulled me in for a kiss. As much as I wanted to resist him and keep arguing my point, it was difficult to do so when his lips were so damn sweet.

I melted into him.

Everything about this man was perfect.

I never should have let him go all those months ago. I should have made more of an effort to mend our relationship instead of letting it crumble to the ground.

As these thoughts filtered through my head, the kiss intensified. His tongue was tangled with mine. They fought against one another but ultimately, Cain came out on top. His victory prize included sucking on the side of my neck and decorating it with a whole trail of bite marks.

"Mmm," he moaned against my skin as his hands dropped down to my ass. He squeezed them and a second later, I was hoisted onto the kitchen table.

"What do you think you're doing?" I was finally able to get my head screwed on straight. "I can't –"

"It's a Sunday, babe. There's no need for you to be working yourself to death. Worrying about the lake isn't going to fix the problem. You're just going to have to trust the lawyers. They know what they're doing."

"And so do I," Axel chimed in. "And sex is the best medicine for an overworked mind." A sly grin painted his face. The two of them were up to something and I wasn't quite sure whether I was ready for it. "Come with me." He beckoned us to follow with a simple bend of his finger. Axel was just that kind of guy. He had the ability to command others – to make them obey. Cain and I were no different.

Now, Axel's mansion was enormous. Even after sleeping there a half dozen times, I barely knew my way around. There were so many different corridors that it was difficult to keep track of it all. I mean, as soon as a house needs an elevator – it's way too big.

But Axel walked with confidence. This was his castle and he was completely comfortable with every single inch.

After what felt like an eternity, we arrived at a luxurious bathroom. The size of it alone compared to that of an average studio apartment. When I say this place was huge, I'm not exaggerating.

Our footsteps echoed against the marble tile.

"Damn..." Cain and I said in unison.

Axel offered a knowing grin as he bent over the Jacuzzi and turned it on.

My eyes instantly gravitated toward the roundness of his ass. Unable to help myself, I stepped forward and groped it. Pressing myself even closer, I allowed him to feel what I was packing.

Meanwhile, Cain was already stripping down. The sight of his lean body had me sprung.

I tugged at the waistband of my pants but the button was being a little bitch. "C'mon, you stupid thing..."

Suddenly, Axel shoved me up against the wall. The impact had me winded. My eyes opened wide as he seemed to tear my clothes right off my body.

"There, that's better," he purred. "Much better."

"Are you guys going to make out or are you going to join me?" Cain was leaning against the Jacuzzi, cock poking out the surface of the water. "Because it is getting awfully lonely in here all by myself."

Axel was quick to abandon me and for good reason too. Cain looked sexy as fuck. Beads of water trailed down his flawless skin. I licked my lips and jumped in next to him. A second later, I had his nipple in my mouth. Axel attacked the other and we both went to town until he was moaning with pleasure.

My tongue flicked all around, back and forth, back and forth. He jerked his hips, body silently begging for more. Feeling generous, I did just that. My hand slipped under the water's surface and grabbed hold of his shaft. With the water acting as lubrication, it was exceptionally easy for me to pleasure my lover. I gave some special attention to his tip. It was no secret that Cain was extremely sensitive in that area. A bit of teasing and he was about ready to lose his mind.

He groaned, eyes rolling into the back of his skull as soon as Axel started fondling his balls. "That feels so good..."

I glanced over at Axel who nodded. We both stopped.

"Why...?" he whimpered.

I silenced him with a kiss. Our lips were made for each other. They danced in perfect harmony, burning fire inside our souls. I fed off that energy and harnessed it against my heart. Yes, our relationship had a good layer of lust but lust wasn't our foundation. We truly cared about one another and I just prayed that it would stay that way for a long, long time.

"Please..." Cain begged.

I kissed him a little harder, trying to get his heart racing. When I saw that enough was enough, I straddled him, guiding his cock into my eager hole. I gasped as soon as his tip popped past my sphincter.

That feels so right, I thought to myself as I eased him further and further inside my depths. Once he was balls deep, I took a moment to adjust myself.

I was about to start moving but before I could do so, Axel took me by the hips. He took full control, bouncing me up and down some other guy's dick. It was a novel experience but one that I quite enjoyed.

Smack!

Somehow, even an underwater smack from this football player still left an impression. I could feel my skin burning as I continued to ride Cain harder and harder.

His balls started to slap against me as the water sloshed all around us.

My toes curled as pleasure coursed through my every inch.

Axel pulled at my hair and looked me in the eye. "Don't you dare cum," he growled. He released my hair. "Switch."

"Huh?" I was in such a sex-induced haze that I couldn't quite understand what he wanted me to do.

Luckily, Cain was quick to action. He slipped out of my ass and flipped us around. He didn't hesitate a single second before he started riding me like a downright cowboy. I had never felt anything quite like it before. My balls tightened and I struggled to keep my composure.

"Please..." I begged. "I'm going to blow.

Axel pulled Cain by the shoulders and bent him over the side of the tub so his cock was dangling right there in front of my face. I didn't need any further instruction as I craned my neck and pulled him into my mouth. My tongue swirled all around his tip while Axel stood up and aligned himself to make the thrust.

Cain screamed as soon as Axel was inside of him. Axel was, by far, the biggest of the three of us and he was merciless with the way he fucked us.

Already, he was going to town on Cain's ass. His whole body jerked with Axel's power.

It was a challenge for me to keep Cain in my mouth without biting down on his shaft.

Axel pulled on his hair and ran his fingernails all down his back, leaving red marks everywhere. Axel was a downright animal.

My tongue traced the underside of Cain's cock. He was really damn close to climaxing. I could see the precum dripping on the edge. I lapped it up and savored the taste. There's a lot of people who think swallowing is gross but I'll never say no to a mouthful of cum. Wanting that to happen, I focused on taking him over the edge. That wasn't very difficult given the fact that Axel was pounding his ass into next week.

Cain clawed at the jacuzzi as he screamed his lungs raw.

"Fuck!" His eyes rolled into the back of his head.

Axel smacked his ass and I swear, I felt it. I shivered and reached down to grab my cock. I stroked it nice and slow until it was as hard as a rock. It was difficult to focus on pleasuring Cain's length when I was so close to a climax of my own.

Suddenly, Cain screamed out louder still and it echoed through the entire bathroom. His body became as stiff as a board as Axel held him in place, balls deep inside Cain's asshole.

A second later, thick, sticky cum came shooting down my throat. I swallowed every last drop, savoring the taste. "Mmm." I grinned up at my lovers.

Axel was breathing hard but by the throbbing of his cock, he had yet to climax. A drop of precum hung on his tip so I leaned forward and lapped it up. He groaned as my tongue circled around his tip and lingered there. I teased him with a back and forth motion. I knew that if I kept it up, he'd be out of his mind.

Before he could pull away from me, I grabbed him by the base of the cock and held him there. Still, I focused on only the tip.

"Oh, you're evil."

"Am I?" I asked innocently. Our eyes locked and I felt a thrill that I could make such a hunk of a man crumble underneath my whim.

My tongue flicked faster and faster.

Axel rocked on his heels, trying to keep with the pleasure.

Cain whistled. "Look at you go," he hollered as I started to take Axel into my mouth. "Swallow that cock." His eyes were bright with excitement as he watched me blow our combined lover.

I hummed ever so slightly so the vibrations could run along his length.

"Fuck," Axel growled as he pulled at my hair. "How did you get so damn good at this?"

His compliment only fueled the fire. I bobbed my head faster and faster, tongue dancing along his underside, trying to find his sweet spot. Once I had it pinpointed, I attacked it with everything I had. To add to Axel's predicament, I started to fondle his balls. My touch was nice and gentle but it was enough to add that little bit more of euphoria.

Axel focused on his breathing.

Damn, this guy has endurance, I thought to myself. What's it going to take to push him over the edge?

I redoubled my efforts, head bobbing at an impossible speed.

Then, just when I thought I had him exactly where I wanted him, he pulled me off his girth. "We're taking this to the bedroom," was all he said before he disappeared.

"You heard the man," Cain said. "The bedroom awaits."

I grinned. "I have a feeling I'm going to like what comes next."

"Oh, no doubt about it." Cain smacked my ass as I got out of the jacuzzi. "How could you not when two of the hottest guys on the planet are fucking your brains out?"

As expected, he tossed me his signature wink and as always, it had me weak in the knees.

Would I ever tire of these men?

The answer was simple.

No.

# Chapter 11: Axel

Was I done with Riley? Not even close. Cain was just the starter and now it was time to move on to the main course and nothing – and I mean nothing – was going to get in my way.

By the time he walked through the door, I already had my cock lubed and ready to go. Oh, I was dying for release – trust me – but I wasn't going to let that get in the way of having my fun.

I beckoned him forward with a curl of my finger. Once he was close enough for me to grab, that's exactly what I did. I pulled him close and turned us around a step so I could put him into one of the bed posts. As soon as I had full control of his body, our lips collided for a full fireworks display. Sparks flew in every direction.

And the best part? Riley was just as hungry for me as I was for him. Who would have thought it would be so damn satisfying to fuck your best friend? Shame on me for friend-zoning him all this time.

My fingers tightened around his wrists, threatening to never let him go. Now, I've had my fair share of fucks but nothing compares to what I've got going on. Cain and Riley? They're the goddamn cherry on the ice-cream sundae and I'm going to do everything in my power to make sure I never fuck this up.

With this thought in mind, I threw him on the bed.

Riley was quick to get into a head down, ass up position. Sometimes, it really does seem like this guy can read my mind.

Seeing his ass on full display, I take a moment to slow down. I run my fingertips along his skin and watch as the goosebumps trickle along the length of his ass. Next, I decorate it with a few kisses, from backbone all the way to his thighs. No inch is left untouched. I wanted him to feel like he was the only man left on the planet and that I was pouring every ounce of my energy into making him feel good.

His soft moans were too much for me. I couldn't hold back any longer. With my hands on his hips, I rammed into his asshole. He was much tighter than Cain and that made the experience ten times better. It was a challenge just to get started and I had used a crap ton of lube. But once I got myself into motion, there was no stopping me.

I went faster and faster until the whole bed threatened to collapse. "That's it, take it, boy!" I growled against his ear as my teeth grazed against the side of his neck. "Take every last inch and take it good."

"Axel..." he groaned my name and his toes curled as his cock twitched. I took it and squeezed it against my palm, squeezing out the cum that was straining for freedom.

"Cum for me," I whispered. "Make a mess on this bed."

And that's exactly what he did. His sperm exploded all over the place. Just seeing the pleasure coursing through his body was enough to push me over the edge. I tried to pull out and coat his back but I was too far gone. My balls unloaded onto his ass, coating every inch of it.

Spent, I pulled out and collapsed onto the edge of the bed.

"Damn, that was hot," Cain said. "My cock is going to be sore for weeks after that wanking session."

"Wanking?" Riley gasped. "What are you, British?"

"I was testing it out. I rather like the word," Cain returned.

The two men bickered it out for a few minutes. It was nice just to hear their voices as I drifted off to sleep.

***

A few hours later.

Ding!

I was awakened by the buzzing of my phone.

What time is it? I thought to myself as I felt around the nightstand, eyes blurry from sleep. Finally, I managed to get my hands on the device. I turned it on and I was instantly blinded by the brightness.

Damnit, why do I always leave it on the highest setting?

Squinting, I struggled to dim the screen. After a bit of fighting with the touch screen, I finally succeeded.

New email! read the notification that had woken me up in the first place.

New email? I thought. Must be important if my phones telling me about it. Everything gets sent to spam these days.

I opened the app and clicked on my inbox. It was an email from my lawyers. The subject line read 'success.'

"Riley!" I shook him a bit too roughly as I shoved my phone in his face. "Look!"

"What?" he mumbled. "Let me sleep for a few more minutes." He tried to roll over but I straddled his body and pinned him in place. "Get off of me. You're crushing my ribs."

"But it's the cease and desist that you were gunning for!" I exclaimed, knowing how excited it would make him. "Wake up, would you?"

He pushed me off and rubbed the sleep from his eyes. "What?"

"Read it."

His eyes widened. "Wait, does this mean what I think it means?"

"What's going on?" Cain propped himself up on his elbow. "Why are you guys making so much noise."

"The lawyers finished filing the cease and desist," I said. "So, if the factory keeps pouring toxic sludge into the lake they are going to be slapped with a pretty hefty penalty."

"That hasn't stopped people in the past," Cain pointed out. "Sometimes it's more cost effective to keep breaking the rules. Basic economics right there."

Riley punched his arm. "There is no need for you to go raining on my parade. This is great news! It's exactly what the lake needed and we couldn't have accomplished it without your lawyers and capital, Axel. I really owe you one."

"You don't owe me anything. That lake means as much to me as it does to you."

Riley blushed and it was the cutest thing I've ever seen. I brushed his burning cheek with the back of my hand.

"Thank you," he whispered.

"Again, you have nothing to thank me for." I kissed the top of his head.

"Hey guys, look at this." Cain interrupted our moment by raising his hand, nearly poking us both in the eye. "Their stock is already plummeting. I guess their investors got wind of this little scandal. At this rate, there's no chance they are going to survive unless they turn around their eco agenda."

"I almost feel bad –"

"Why?" I asked, cutting Riley off.

"Well, I didn't want to bring them down to financial ruin."

"Even after what they did – after they endangered a whole ecosystem?" I asked. "You're just going to let them off the hook?"

"I'm not letting them off the hook." He looked up and caught my eye. "I just don't think that anyone should be cut down to their knees like that. I would have liked it better if they still had a leg to stand on."

"And this is why you have a heart made of gold." I took his hands and squeezed them against mine. "And the reason why I love you."

"L-Love?" It sounded like he was choking on the word.

"Yes, love," I affirmed. "And it may seem like I am saying this way too soon in our relationship but I just can't help the fact that you two make me feel this way." I looked over at Cain and took his hand. "You two fill up a part in my heart that I never knew was empty and I can't thank you enough for that."

A great big grin painted Cain's face. He wrapped his arms around my body. "I love you too, big boy."

Riley was the last to say it but those three magical words left his lips too and it was the best moment of my life.

# Chapter 12: Riley

Five months later, February.

"Fuck, it's cold." Despite the layers I wore, the frigid winter air still penetrated down to my skin, turning it to ice. "Why couldn't they have made the venue someplace... warmer."

"It's the Superbowl, quit your bitching and support your man." Cain took me by the hand and pulled me through the bleachers. The place was packed up to the rafters. Everyone was wearing their team colors and I was one of them.

"Also, how come jerseys cost an arm and a leg? It's ridiculous."

Cain rolled his eyes. "You aren't going to keep this up the whole game, are you?"

"Depends how cold it gets. Maybe my lips will freeze together."

"Here's hoping for that."

I shot him a stare of death but by doing so, I lost track of my footing and tripped on one of the steps. I was sure I was going down but then a pair of strong arms steadied me. I looked up and there he was – the man of my dreams – or, at least, one of them – Cain. His eyes sparkled against the sunlight.

My breath hitched against the back of my throat. I couldn't believe I had managed to snag such a looker. Even after months of waking up by his side, it was still difficult to accept that I would no longer need to keep on living on my own. Loneliness was a stranger now.

"Always the clumsy one," he said with a chuckle. "Come on, let's get to our seats before you break your neck."

Thanks to Axel's smooth talking we'd managed to snag some of the best seats in the stadium. As a kid playing in his high school football team, I had only ever dreamed of watching the Superbowl this close to the field. I'd be able to see every play – every tackle – every spike of the ball – and you'd best believe that I was pumped.

"So, I've been reading up on the teams and our opponent has some pretty nasty stats. By sheer numbers alone, their set to beat us."

I rammed my elbow into his ribs. "Cain!"

"Ouch! What was that for?"

"Jinxing us," I said. "You can't come here and say that we're going to lose."

"I didn't say we were going to lose," he protested. "I just said that the numbers are telling me –"

"Well, maybe you should stop listening to the numbers because I think they are telling you lies. We're going to win this."

"Numbers don't lie."

"Don't test my patience, Cain," I warned. "Or, did you forget that I used to be a football player myself?"

"Forget? How do you think I could forget when I get to see that body each and every night?" His voice took a soft and seductive tone.

"Not now," I hissed.

"Oh?" he mused like he was the most innocent man on the planet. "What's wrong?"

"You know –"

Suddenly, the whole stadium hushed into a state of quiet. Just like everyone else, I inched toward the edge of my seat. I held my breath as I waited for something to happen.

And bang!

The entire team came rushing from the locker room, guns blazing. Axel was at the head of the pack looking like he was ready to take down the world. I feared for anyone who dared to step in his path.

"He's going to be an animal tonight," I whispered in Cain's direction.

"Oh, no doubt about it. Would you look at that expression he's wearing? It's like he's a warrior about to fight a war."

"That's because this is war."

"That's a little dramatic, don't you think?" Cain had a much more nonchalant approach to football. He wasn't a fanatic like Axel and me.

He would sit down and watch the game, sure, but he wasn't crazy about it.

"This is the Superbowl – everything's on the line. If Axel doesn't win this, it could be the end of his career."

"And then bye-bye nice mansion." Cain frowned. "I really hope he wins this..."

"Oh, so now you want us to win?"

"I never said I didn't."

"Yeah, yeah, tell it to the judge."

Our bickering was put to an end when a tall black woman walked up to the mic stand and started to sing the national anthem. I kept my hand over my heart and my head bowed in silence. Beside me, Cain was singing along. His voice was soft and sweet as it wafted through the air all around me and warmed it a few degrees.

The stadium erupted with applause.

"She was good," I commented.

"Really good," Cain agreed. "Let's just hope that Axel can follow in her footsteps."

"You know he will. Axel came here ready to play."

***

By halftime, we were massacring the other team. They didn't stand a chance.

"Things are looking good," Cain said.

"I think he has this thing in the bag."

"Don't count your chickens before they hatch," he warned. "Anything can happen during the second half. You tell me that all the time."

"You're right but I have a feeling that Axel is going to show the whole world exactly what he's made of tonight."

"But first we get to see what that guy is made of." Cain pointed at the musician that had just taken his shirt off. A couple of wild fan girls were practically throwing fists at one another in an attempt to grab it and keep it for themselves.

"Are you... drooling?" I asked when I glanced over at Cain and saw him completely fixated.

"What? No!" he said much too quickly. "I was just... uh, admiring his... tattoos. Yeah, that's it."

"You're such a horrible liar."

"Sorry."

There was a bitterness in my mouth as I considered the fact that Cain was attracted to the man on stage.

Then, he took my hand and laced our fingers together. "You know there's nothing for you to worry about, right? That guy's a celebrity. Never in a million years would he look my way and even if he did, I wouldn't look back because I already have the men of my dreams by my side."

His words made me blush. "Do you really mean that?"

"I wouldn't have said it if I didn't mean it. I love you, Riley, and don't you ever forget that."

***

It was down to the last minute. Somehow, the opposing team had managed to catch up when our defense took a nose dive into Shitsville. Now the score was in their favor.

"Come on, don't let this slip between your fingers, Axel. You can do this." My words sounded like a prayer as I hung on to the railing in front of me, knuckles turning white. "You can't lose."

The clock ticked away.

What are you doing? screamed that voice at the back of my head. Throw the damn ball!

And that's when the football went flying. It rolled from his fingertips and pierced through the wind. For a second there, it wobbled. Its speed was affected and I feared the running back wouldn't take that into consideration.

Sack!

Axel was tackled to the ground. I lost track of the ball, too concerned with the well-being of my boyfriend. A collective gasp rose from the crowd. The commentator was screaming something into the mic but his words were impossible to understand.

"Can you see? Can you see?" Cain was holding onto my sleeve for dear life. "What's going on? Are we going to make it to the endzone?"

I blinked and saw the moment of truth.

"Touchdown!" Like thousands of others, I rose to my feet, screaming my head off.

"We did it?" Cain asked. "We did it!" He bounced along with me as the clock wound down to zero. That was it, we were Superbowl champions.

The excitement did not ebb away. I was filled with pride as Axel held that giant trophy over his head, his lips stretching from ear to ear.

"Is there anything you'd like to say to America?" the reporter asked as she held up the mic to Axel's lips.

He took it from her and started walking in our direction. "Yes, I would." His voice was ragged and breathless. "First and foremost, I would like to thank two special people in my life. They are the most unlikely of partners but they've been the best choice I've ever made." His eyes locked with mine and it sent a shiver running through my spine. "I know most of you know me as a playboy but those days are over."

Whispered gossip rose up as people tried to decipher his words.

Cain squeezed my hand.

"I've never been put on such a spotlight like this before," he said.

"Well, you better smile because the whole world is watching," I whispered out of the corner of my mouth.

Axel stopped so he was standing right in front of us. "And I want everyone to know that you should never hold yourself back just because you're scared. Don't let that fear control you because it might be preventing you from the best damn moments of your life." He dropped the mic and pulled us both into a tight embrace.

It felt like my heart was going to fly right out of my chest. My face burned as every single person stared at our threesome. But what did I care? Axel and Cain both made me happy and that's what mattered most.

"I love you," Axel whispered. "And thank you for pushing me to become my very best. I couldn't have made it this far without you two."

# Epilogue: Axel

A few years later.

"It's been a pleasure, coach." I dropped an envelope on his desk.

"What's this?"

"Well, my contract is coming to a close and I've decided that I'm going into early retirement."

"Early retirement?" he repeated. "But you've won the Superbowl for three straight years."

"And I'd rather get out while I'm still ahead."

"You'll be letting a lot of people down, including myself," he said. "Are you sure you want to do this?"

"You can waste your breath and try to convince me otherwise but it's not going to work. I've already made up my mind."

"And there's no way –"

I shook my head. "I have a family that I need to take care of and being away from home all the time, it isn't a life I want to have any more. As you know, we just adopted a little boy. I want to be there for him."

"And you don't think he would be proud to have a daddy that goes into the football hall of fame? That'll only happen if you keep on trucking."

"It won't matter if he never gets to see me," I countered. "I want to be there to read him bedtime stories and to make him breakfast in the morning. I can't do that as effectively if I'm married to the sport."

The coach sighed. "You're a stubborn one, Axel. I know that from experience. I wish I could keep you but if your mind is set – it's set."

"Thank you for understanding." I nodded my head and left the office. It was the last time I'd walk through that locker room. The feeling was bittersweet but deep down, I knew I was making the right decision.

***

When I arrived home, I was immediately greeted by Missy. As always, she jumped on her hind legs and practically drowned me in a bath of kisses. I tried to push her away but she was persistent.

Then came the baby. He had already learned how to crawl and he was a fast, little bugger. Quick as lightning, he clung to my leg and looked up with those great blue eyes of his. "Hey there, Junior, what are you doing out here all on your own? Where're your daddies?"

"There he is!" Riley huffed from the doorway. "I thought I had lost him for a minute."

"Is everything alright?" I asked, raising an eyebrow in question.

"Well, he needs his diaper changed but he keeps running away from me and he's a hard one to catch."

"I'll handle it." I took the clean diaper from his hand and walked down the hall to the nursery. "You need to stop giving Daddy Riley such a hard time." I wagged my finger at Junior who decided it was a pretty good teething toy.

I chuckled. It was hard to stay mad at a baby when they were so damn cute.

"Now, you be a good boy for me, you hear?"

The baby gurgled and slapped my face with his slobber-coated hand. Oh, the joys of being a parent.

***

"How did it go in there?" Riley asked as soon as I walked into the kitchen.

"Crisis averted," I said. "No more stinky diaper." I placed our son in his playpen and then went over to both Riley and Cain to give them a kiss. "So, what are you cooking, good looking?" I slapped Cain's ass making him jump a little. "Because whatever it is, it smells divine."

"Sweet garlic chicken and green beans."

"Damn," I whistled. "That sounds amazing. Tell me again why you decided to be a stock broker instead of a cook?"

"I like numbers more."

"There's something wrong with you," I teased.

"Tell me about it," Riley added. "I've been trying to figure that out for years." He was busy setting the table and even doing something so simple as that, he looked hot as hell. I thought that my attraction for these guys would fade with time – as all things do – but it was as strong as ever. Some days, it was just as hot as it was back when we first started dating.

"I have big news to share with everyone."

"Oh?" Riley and Cain said in unison.

"We'll discuss it over dinner," I said.

"Well, dinner is served." Cain divided up the meal into three even portions. Steam rolled off the meal. My stomach flip-flopped, unable to wait another moment.

"Wine, anyone?" I was already reaching for the bottle.

"Me," Riley said.

"I'll pass," came Cain's response. "Just water."

"Water?"

"I'm trying to watch my figure," he said.

"Who are you kidding?" I poured him a glass of wine and practically shoved it into his hand. "There's nothing for you to watch. You're just as hot as you've always been and don't you start thinking otherwise. I don't need you going on some fad diet again. That was a nightmare."

"It worked."

"For as long as you kept up with it," I countered. "Then you gained back everything you lost."

He frowned.

"All I'm trying to say is that you're perfect just the way you are."

We all sat down and picked at our food. "So, are you going to tell us what this big announcement is?" Riley had always been the impatient one.

"Right." I cleared my throat. "I have decided to retire."

"Retire?" Riley nearly choked on his food. "What do you mean, retire?"

"I've given up football."

"Why would you do that?" Cain asked, looking flabbergasted.

"Because I want to spend more time with Junior and I can't do that if I'm always on the field."

"Are you sure this is a good idea?" Riley asked.

"I'll stay home and take care of him."

"So, you're going to be a stay-at-home dad?" Cain cocked his head like I had just sprouted tentacles from my shoulders.

"That's right."

"Well, if that's what you want to do, I'm not going to stop you," Riley said. "And, I'm actually quite proud of you for giving up something you love so much to raise your son."

"Life is full of responsibilities and its time I own up to that. I've had my fun and now its time to grow up and raise the family I've always wanted." I flashed them both a smile. "Here's to the rest of our lives." I clinked my glass against theirs knowing this was the start of something truly beautiful.

*****

*****

# Don't miss out!

Visit the website below and you can sign up to receive emails whenever Van Cole publishes a new book. There's no charge and no obligation.

https://books2read.com/r/B-A-RTRV-XQPCC

**BOOKS 2 READ**

Connecting independent readers to independent writers.

# Also by Van Cole

3 Man Huddle: MMM Best Friend Romance
His Alpha Wolf: Gay First Time Romance
A Dragon's Miracle: Gay Dragon MPREG Romance
Double-Teamed: MMM First Time Football Romance
His Football Star: Gay Second Chance Romance
Love In My Town: MM First Time Romance
Training A Hockey Star
Game Night
Double Shift
Take A Shot
Dear Professor
Getting Inked
Ninth Inning
Triple Threat
Seducing My Best Friend's Brother
My Protector
The Blueprint
Show Me The Way
End Zone
Matched To His Tiger
Love At First Puck
My Straight Boss
Falling For The Alpha
My Boss
On Thin Ice